PROMISES

Gamerhate
by Tony Lee
Illustrated by Georgina Fearns
Published by Ransom Publishing Ltd.
Unit 7, Brocklands Farm, West Meon, Hampshire GU32 1JN, UK
www.ransom.co.uk

ISBN   978 178591 320 4
First published in 2016

Tony Lee

Ransom

1

DethKilla thought he had me dead in his sights.

But he was wrong.

I'd been playing him along, waiting for the right moment to take my shot.

And the moment I did, it was beautiful.

He took the blast straight to the body, collapsing lifeless to the ground.

And a second later, the messages started to come through.

> AWESOME SHOT DUDE!

> MDK TO THE FACE!

I sat back and watched the messages with a smile.

DethKilla deserved everything that came to him.

He'd been a pain in the neck for pretty much everyone on the server. He preferred to player-kill rather than co-op.

Not cool.

Now he'd received the same as he gave out – and he wasn't happy.

> CHEAT SHOT SNEAK
PLAYING SUCKS

'But you do it all the time,' I said, as I typed the words in reply. 'How's it feel to be beaten by a girl?'

The moment I pressed **SEND**, I knew I'd made a mistake.

In fact, I'd broken the one big rule for all girl players:

Don't tell them you're a girl.

It wasn't like I played wearing a fake beard or anything, or said I was a boy in any of my profile details.

Even my gamertag, **CYBERUN1C0RN**, was as far from '*Grr! I'm a boy!*' as I could get.

But I'd never said I *wasn't* a boy. And anyway, over the last couple of weeks I'd made some good online friends here.

Friends who suddenly realised that they were being taken down pretty easily by a *fourteen-year-old girl*.

>   NO WAY U R A GIRL

>   GO BAK TO UR DOLLIES

And, just like that, I knew that my time on this server was over.

Pulling off my headset, I stared at the monitor screen as more and more one-line messages of sexism and abuse came through.

How *dare* I lie to them! (I hadn't lied.) They were sick of carrying me on missions! (I'd killed more targets then most of them combined.)

And then there were the messages I always seemed to get the moment my identity as a girl was revealed ...

> RU PRTTY? I DATE U

> BET U KISS BETTER THAN U SHOOT

> BAK OFF BRO I ASK 1ST

> SHE DON WANT U SHE WAN ME

And there I was, watching teenage boys turning into nothing more than cavemen in the space of two minutes.

I sighed and signed out of the server.

It was always the same. They were quite happy for a girl to play their game, until the moment that the girl proved herself their equal.

Or – shock horror – proved to be *better* than them.

Annoyed, I lay on my bed and put my earphones in.

Maybe I'd try an American server next time.

Maybe *they'd* be less idiotic.

2

'I told you, it's always going to be that way. Boys close ranks when there's an invasion.'

Kyle bit into his sandwich and stared back at me. 'It's what they do.'

'I don't think a girl playing their game counts as an invasion,' I replied, as I searched through my own packed lunch for something that looked even remotely edible. 'They just need to grow up.'

Kyle spluttered as he sipped at his drink.

' "Teenage boys."

' "Grow up."

'Those are two phrases that will *never* go well together.'

I laughed as we continued to eat lunch.

Kyle was probably the only boy in the school that accepted me for what I was.

He didn't try to buttonhole me into a particular slot.

I was pretty, with long dark hair.

In most boy's worlds, I should be dating the captain of the football team and following pop bands and singers.

I should be hanging around with friends and having sleepovers and stuff.

I didn't know exactly what these boys thought I should do, because I simply wasn't wired that way.

Sure, I had dolls. But they were American collector figures, still mint in their boxes.

NOT to be played with!

I loved music, but I was a bit less boy band and more 'tortured soul' in my tastes.

And the last thing I wanted to do was date 'pretty boys' or hang around in a girly gang.

Unless that gang was working out the stats of the next server raid.

Or handing out roles and ammunition to each player.

No, I was too much of a tomboy for
the girls, and too much of a girl for the
boys.

'So, yes or no?'

Kyle was watching me, and
I realised that I hadn't heard a word
that he'd said.

I smiled sheepishly.

'Sorry, what?' I replied.

'Are you gonna try for the trophy?'
he repeated. 'I mean, Craig Scotton won

last year and he's terrible. It'd be a walkover for you.'

'I don't know, it's being run by Mr French this year, and he's ... *difficult.*'

I stood up, packing my rubbish into my rucksack.

'In fact, I was going to see him this lunch. So I'll see you in class.'

The trophy that Kyle had mentioned

was the School Gamer Trophy. It was given each year to the winning finalist of a player-verses-player shoot 'em-up.

For the last three years Craig Scotton, or **DethKilla,** had won it easily.

But after shooting him easily the night before, I reckoned I had a good chance to beat him this year.

But Mr French was known to hate gaming. Plus he was very old-fashioned in his beliefs.

He'd been given the job of

organising the competition this year
because the usual organiser, Mrs Lucas,
was on maternity leave.

It was only open to Years 9 to 11,
and this was the first year that I was
old enough to enter.

I knew I had a good chance of being
the first girl ever to win.

But as I walked towards Mr French
in the hallway, I could see from his face
that he knew why I was coming. And I
knew what his answer was going to be.

'I'm sorry, but I put a halt on your Unicorn thingie name tag,' he said, before I'd even spoken a word. 'You're frozen from entering.'

I was shocked at his flat refusal.

'Why?'

'No girls this year,' he said, turning to walk away. 'Go do home economics, or something more … *ladylike*.'

'That's unfair!' I shouted. 'Girls have always been allowed to enter!'

Mr French turned back to me. 'That's true. And every year they've been destroyed by the other players,' he said.

'Face it, Becky. I'm doing this for your own good. Girls simply aren't cut out for gaming at this level.'

I fought down the tears that came to my eyes.

At that moment I knew two things: I would win, and I would prove all my critics wrong.

All I had to do was enter a game

I was barred from playing in, beat everyone without them realising I was a girl, and win the trophy.

3

In a way, it was easier than I thought it would be.

Because of bandwidth issues for the

early stages, the rules said that players could log into the server from their own machines.

So, for much of the gaming, I could play from home. Nobody would find out who I was.

The only problem would be the final, as the school always made a big thing about it. They always brought in the local press and turned it into a big event.

There was no way I could get out of being seen at the final, but by that point I'd be one of four remaining players. I'd cross that bridge when I came to it.

The other problem was **DethKilla**, or Craig Scotton. He might not know who **CYBERUN1C0RN** was, but he knew now that she was a girl.

If I went in under my usual tag, the chances were that he'd ensure all the other players teamed up on me, or worse – he'd tell Mr French *there was a girl in the game.*

As I logged onto my gamertag,
I realised I'd probably have to change
my name for the competition …

I stopped as I stared at my profile
screen. It wasn't how I left it.

It was filled with abusive messages,
pictures of Barbie dolls and small girls
skipping.

I'd been *hacked*.

The same boys who I'd beaten in the
games had now returned the favour.

They'd broken into my account and completely trashed it.

I could see they'd even played as me online, using my gamertag to flirt with other players.

This was bad.

I was crushed. If he didn't know who **CYBERUN1C0RN** was before now, Craig would definitely know it was me by now.

There was no way I could enter the contest.

I sat back, and for the first time in ages, I started to cry.

I wasn't crying because I wasn't allowed to play.

I was crying because of the hurtful things that complete strangers had said and done to me, simply because I was a girl.

When I showed it to Kyle, he went ballistic.

I think if I hadn't stopped him, he would have hunted the school for whoever did it.

And that would have been crazy, because it was only by random chance that Craig was even on the server.

Most of the players were from Europe and had never met me.

I think that was one of the reasons why Kyle was so angry.

'You have to stop this,' he said at school. 'It'll get worse. They'll doxx you, put your name and address, all your details up on the net. They'll throw you out to the crazies. I've seen it done.'

'I'm not stopping,' I snapped back. 'They won't beat me. I won't let them.'

'Then you're an idiot,' Kyle said simply, as I got up and walked away from him.

I wasn't angry with *him*. He was still trying to protect me, and actually I found that attractive in him.

But I wasn't going to go down without a fight.

As I walked to my next lesson, Craig strolled past me, smiling as he aimed his fingers at me like guns.

'*Pew pew pew*, Unicorn,' he whispered.

A shiver ran down my back, and I hurried on, not sure what I should do.

As it was, the next lesson was English, and it couldn't have been timed better, as we worked on William Shakespeare's *The Merchant of Venice*.

And, as the lesson went on, I learned about the main character, Portia, and how she dressed as a man to outwit the bad guy Shylock.

And as Mr Williams talked about all kinds of stuff to do with the play, I stared at the floor.

Then it hit me.

I had a plan to outwit my own Shylock. I would enter the school gaming contest as a *boy*.

4

In the early stages of the contest a lot
of players didn't let on who they were.

This was OK because teachers were

afraid of players being bullied in the earlier rounds – especially new gamers who might not be very good.

So all I needed to do was create a new account and use the school's server password to log in.

In half an hour I'd created a new Year 9 male student gamertag for myself: **K1LLSW1TCH.**

No details, no information – except for the fact that I was a boy – and a password that would take a genius to hack.

I was ready.

Kyle suggested I didn't enter the contest, but I ignored him. I was in 'full gamer mode' now, and nothing would stop me.

And, in the first two qualifying rounds, I played from home and utterly shredded my rivals.

I realised at the end of the second round that I was the only player left in who hadn't given out their real name – and the school had picked up on it.

People were asking each other, 'Are you **Killswitch**?' during lessons.

But nobody ever asked me.

So I sat back and watched, feeling smug and knowing that, for the moment, nobody could touch me.

And I was the same in the games. I was on fire, as if being this unknown male student had somehow released me from my usual, calmer gaming style.

I took risks, I played loose with the rules of the game, and still I won.

By the time we reached the fourth and final qualifying round, I was in second place, behind Scott.

I had been watching his own matches on the screen – and I knew, without a doubt, that if we had played each other in any of the qualifying games, I would now be first.

I would have taken him down before he could spawn fully.

DethKilla was in my crosshairs again, and this time I was taking no prisoners.

It was really funny to see the other players stress out on who I was.

I admit it – I enjoyed winding them up! I even created a blog under the gamertag **K1LLSW1TCH** that dished dirt on them.

Yes, it was mind games, but for the first time they were mind games being played under *my own* rules.

And every night when I logged on as **K1LLSW1TCH**, I could see where other players had tried to hack into my profile, desperately trying to learn who I was.

I felt powerful.

I felt empowered.

I felt *sick*.

Because I knew that eventually,
I was going to have to come clean and
tell everyone who I was.

And that would probably lead to me
being kicked out of the contest. And
maybe even suspended from school.

After all, I was really pretending to
be a different student.

The day that the finalists were named in assembly, I almost threw up in fear.

Me, Craig Scotton, Amir Khan and Billy Murray. (Of course, my real name wasn't given.)

Mr French came on stage and explained that the final would be played the following morning. The whole school would get lessons off to come and cheer on their favourite players.

I looked across at Kyle. He was right after all.

I couldn't do this. I had to step down. I had to bow out of the contest.

At the end of assembly I ran to the nurse, complaining of cramps. I got her to send me home.

If I was off sick, then it wasn't a failure, right? Yeah. I'd be sick. Can't win if you're off sick.

But the next morning, my Mum kicked me out of bed and forced me to school.

It was almost as if she knew. (Later on, I learned that she did know, because Kyle had told her.)

And Kyle waited for me at the gates as I arrived.

'You have to do this,' he said.

'You've changed your tune,' I replied.

Kyle shrugged.

'You're not one to stop, to quit,' he carried on. 'You're a fighter. Its one of the reasons I … well … one of the reasons I really like you.'

He blushed as he spoke, and there was a flutter in my chest.

For the first time the flutter wasn't nerves at my playing in the final.

It was the fact that I liked him too, and this had finally forced us to admit it.

I smiled, holding his hand as we walked into the assembly hall with the other students.

I knew he was right. All I had to do was tell the truth.

On the stage were four desks, each with a gaming PC on it. Three of the four finalists sat waiting.

One space was empty. The school was waiting for the mysterious **K1LLSW1TCH** to arrive.

Taking a deep breath, I walked up to the stage.

Mr French stared down at me.

'Yes?'

'It's me, sir. I'm **Killswitch**.'

There was a hiss of noise, as the students closest to me passed on what they'd heard to the rows behind.

I looked up at Mr French, and saw the anger in his eyes.

'That's a shame,' he said. 'Because you're banned.'

5

The hall went wild as Mr French stared down at me.

'I told you that you weren't allowed

to enter, but you did so anyway,' he said. 'So you're definitely out. Now we'll have just a three-way final.'

'That's not fair!' I cried, looking across at Craig Scotton, who was laughing as he watched me. 'I played better than anyone else here! You've got no excuse to do this!'

'I have every excuse,' Mr French replied. 'Girls shouldn't play – '

There was a bubbling of angry noise from the hall, cutting Mr French off.

The girls of the school, many of them gamers themselves, were angry. And they were getting noisy.

Mr French tried to calm the noise, waving everyone down.

'You can complain all you like,' he said, as the noise finally settled. 'But I'm running this competition, and my word is law – '

'I think you'll find it isn't.'

The lone, female voice echoed around the hall, and I turned to see Mrs

Lucas, her new-born baby in a pushchair beside her.

Mr French went white as she walked towards the stage.

'I've run this contest for five years, and a player has **NEVER** been excluded because of their sex,' she said. 'I think it sends a bad message to the press we have here, don't you, Mr French?'

Mr French stared across at the photographers, already taking photos of us.

'But she can't be allowed to carry on,' he replied. 'She was pretending to be somebody else when she played.'

'Because you *made* her.'

'I didn't do anything.'

Mr French looked around, as if he was looking for someone to save him. 'It's the rules.'

Mrs Lucas turned to me. 'Did you play using your own gamertag?' she asked.

I shook my head. No.

'It was hacked, and Mr French froze it from the contest.'

'*Frozen*, not removed?'

I smiled. I saw where she was going.

Mrs Lucas turned to face the school.

'Becky Lynch can play the final under her usual tag of **Cyber Unicorn**,' she said, to a massive cheer from the crowd.

As the deafening noise echoed around, she looked back to me.

'You ready for this?' she asked.

I nodded, trembling.

'Then take your seat.'

I sat down at the spare PC, facing Craig, who wasn't smiling any more.

He knew that suddenly there was a very real, very *female* threat to his winning streak.

I looked across the hall, seeing the students cheering my name.

'U–NI–CORN! U–NI–CORN!'

It echoed around the hall as I looked to the grinning Kyle.

I winked, cracked my knuckles and turned back to my screen.

I *could* win this.

And I *did*.

More great reads in the Promises series

I ♥ Glitter Boy
by Julia Clark

Lily loves bling - and she loves Mark Ward too. He just doesn't know it yet.

But he will, as soon as he opens her love letter to him, filled with shiny pink glitter.

Can Lily win Glitter Boy's heart?

I Love My Friend's Guy
by Kathryn White

Abi and Erica are from two completely different backgrounds, but they have the same problem: they're in love with their best friend's boyfriend.

Talking to each other online helps, but can Abi and Erica each survive their own heartache? And what will happen when they meet up?

MORE GREAT READS
IN THE PROMISES SERIES

Picture Him

by Jo Cotterill

Aliya loves taking photos. She talks with a stammer, but who needs words when you have pictures?

But when Aliya looks at her latest series of photos ('zombie princess', taken with her friend Zoe) she sees a murky figure in the background of many of them. Is she being stalked?

My Sister's Perfect Husband

by Rosemary Hayes

Laila's older sister Mina is eighteen, and her Pashtun family feel it's time they found her a husband.

They introduce her to several suitable young men, but Mina scowls at each one, putting them off as much as she can.

So Laila sets about finding the perfect husband for her sister.